In a Village by the Sea

By Muon Van
Illustrated by April Chu

Text copyright © 2015 Muon Van
Illustrations copyright © 2015 April Chu
Book design by Simon Stahl

Published by Creston Books, LLC
www.crestonbooks.co

Source of Production: Worzalla Books, Stevens Point, Wisconsin
Printed and bound in the United States of America
1 2 3 4 5

For my father
– MV

For Dan San Souci
– AC

In a fishing village by the sea
there is a small house.

In that house,
high above the waves,
is a kitchen.

In that kitchen
is a bright,
glowing fire.

In that fire
is a pot
of steaming noodle soup.

By that soup
sits a woman,
watching and stirring.

By that woman
is a sleepy child,
yawning and turning.

By that child,
tucked in the shadows,
is a dusty hole.

In that hole
is a brown cricket,
humming and painting.

In that painting
is a sudden storm,
roaring and flashing.

In that storm
is a white boat,
crashing and rolling.

In that boat
is a fisherman,
hoping the storm will end soon,

because in his village
by the sea

there is a small house,

and in that house
is a family
waiting for him to come home.